FOOD FOR
THOUGHT

"A spectacular rendition of a classic tale we only thought we knew. Ferrante's *Food for Thought* weaves a riveting narrative of love and loyalty, grief and hunger, and adds new dimension to the goddesses and gods of Ancient Greece. This is a retelling you won't want to put down!"

—MJ Pankey, author of *Epic of Helinthia*

FOOD FOR THOUGHT

by Ariana Ferrante

Brigids Gate
PRESS

Food for Thought

Edited by: MJ Pankey
Proofed and formatted by: Stephanie Ellis
Cover illustration and design by: Elizabeth Leggett

First Edition: November 2023

ISBN (paperback): 978-1-957537-85-6
ISBN (ebook): 978-1-957537-84-9
Library of Congress Control Number: 2023947547

BRIGIDS GATE PRESS
Bucyrus, Kansas
www.brigidsgatepress.com

Printed in the United States of America

To those who have ever yearned for what they could not have

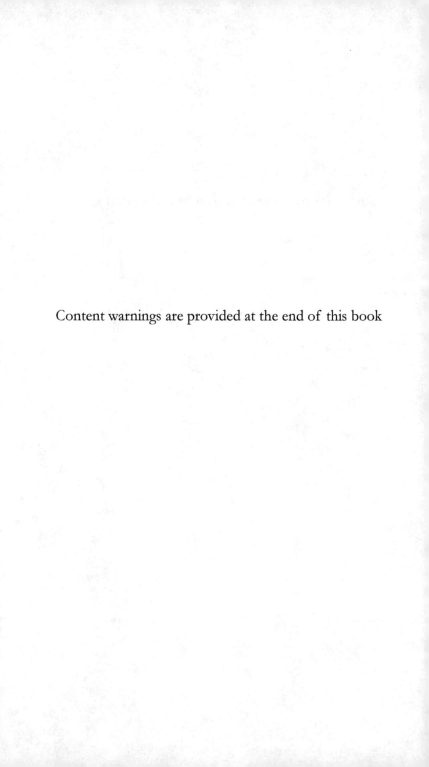

Content warnings are provided at the end of this book

Food for Thought

No one came to Limos for kindness.

She dealt only in cruelty, conversed only with the terrible and desperate. No kind man wished another to starve, and no kind man came to demand favors from the goddess of famine to ensure that wish came true. Only the worst of mortals sought her aid.

Her abode was not easy to reach. Though she wasn't certain how many attempted to request her services in person, she knew enough from those scant few that did appear that the surrounding area unnerved them. She and her land were equal parts neglected—an even stretch of bare, lifeless land along a tall mountainside, sticking out among the greenery like a bald spot on an aged man. What few trees stood in the vicinity were dried up and bent, roots nestled weakly in the cracked, dusty earth. Her house, if it could even be called that, was an otherwise windowless hole carved into the mountain's stony face, sealed over by a slab of rotted wood.

Limos felt the dust shift beneath crunching footsteps, and her sunken eyes cracked open. Someone was coming.

Sitting up, she turned her attention to her poor excuse for a door. It was morning, and shafts of light pierced through the hole-riddled slab to alert her to such a fact.

No sooner had she made a mental note to replace the door than a hollow knock sounded against it. Limos froze, the noise stunning her. Only rarely did anyone ever knock. Usually, they kept their distance and shouted, yearning to call her out of her home like they would an animal from deep hibernation. *This person is daring*, she thought.

She wanted to see how daring he would be once he came face to face with her.

Loosing her bony limbs from beneath her meager covers, Limos crawled out of bed and stood. Rising to her hunched height, she closed the short distance between her cot and the door. "Who is it?" she asked, voice creaking and hoarse.

"Anakletos of Lerna. I have come to seek your aid."

A laugh caught in her skinny throat. "Not much aid to be found here, Anakletos of Lerna," Limos said.

"For destruction, then."

The corners of her cracked lips curled upwards. "Destruction. *Destruction*, I can do." Grabbing the edge of the rotted slab, she pushed the door open, finding Anakletos already pale-faced and trembling.

The sight of her tore a small cry from his throat, and Limos refused to hide her mirth. He'd come all this way—it would have been rude of her to hide her face. Now he could see every inch of her terrible shape, the visage of the goddess he sought. He could see how her snarled, earth-brown hair hung loosely to her too-slim waist. He could see the sunken black eyes of her age-lined face, how they sat above protruding cheekbones, and how her jutting, sharp, curved nose like a carrion bird stood above her peeling lips.

"Who do you request I pay a visit?" she asked.

Anakletos did not respond for a long moment. He merely stared, knees threatening to knock together. Finally, he cleared his throat and forced the words from his lips. "Karpos. My neighbor. His trees are bursting with life and his cows provide milk in excess! Mine are far less prosperous."

Limos wrinkled her nose. "And you come to me to kill his trees and cattle and not Demeter to make yours bear fruit and milk?" The goddess's name dropped from her lips with a snarl; she was the goddess of harvest and growth. Limos was the goddess of famine and hunger. No two deities were more opposed, their dichotomous powers so great that the Fates themselves ordered them never to meet.

Anakletos shook his head, the motion so swift that his features blurred. "He owns more land than I," he explained. "While my farmland is productive, his overshadows me. I can never sell as much as him."

"Money," Limos said, scowling. She knew she'd find the culprit eventually.

"If he sells less, I sell more. And if I sell more, my family lives comfortably. I have but one daughter, and she is young and ill. She needs more food than I can provide!"

Limos paused at his pleas. *Not money then*, she thought, *not completely*. A family, a *daughter*. Her nostrils flared with a huff. Limos was unfamiliar and ignorant to the joys of creation. She was born into the world barren and unfruitful in every sense. The ease of humanity to produce life when she, a goddess, could not made her sick with jealousy. But if there was no life, there was nothing for her to starve. If there was nothing for her to starve, there would be no sacrifices and the feeling of power that came with it. It was a selfish desire, and she knew it, but no more selfish than any other request that came her way.

"And what have you to give me," she began, "if I decimate his farmland?"

"I have a sheep I could give you," Anakletos said. "And libations of milk and wine. The sheep is neither young nor fast, but—"

The goddess waved her bony fingers. "I care not whether your sacrifice is healthy or not," Limos retorted. "Hunger is no selective affliction. Even the greatest king still feels its pangs at times. The sheep is satisfactory. Sacrifice it whole in my name and your neighbor's farm will suffer. This I promise you."

Anakletos bowed his head, eyes trained on the broken, dusty earth. "It will be done as soon as I return home."

Limos grabbed the side of her door. "See to it." Without another word she closed it, the young man's departing footsteps quieting into distant silence.

The sheep arrived as promised days later. It appeared on the goddess's land in a cloud of rising dust, the disturbed grains clearing to reveal its bloodless body. Limos crouched over the sheep's corpse, watching the milk and wine run down its unmoving frame in minute rivers. The liquid formed a murky outline around the animal, dampening the barren soil for the first time in months.

Limos dipped onto her knees, tucking her tattered clothes beneath her as she loomed over the corpse. "It will be done," she echoed, and began to tear, piling limb upon limb past her unhinging jaws.

She took to the skies once finished, flitting to Lerna within the hour. She touched down as a cloud of shapeless dust, materializing as she stepped over drying soil. Her bare feet left a spreading trail of dry grass and withering vines, bringing her across the homestead toward the orchard of budding fruit trees. Limos brushed her fingertips against the bark and watched it peel in famished retreat from her touch. She left no tree unhungry, their branches sagging and sad in her wake, the leaves starting to scatter from neglect.

Before she dissolved to dust again, Limos made certain to wave in the direction of Anakletos.

It was quiet for several days after that. No man or woman came for her assistance, whether in person or otherwise. She sat alone on her land, knees hugged to her chest as she watched the dust dance in the wind.

She waved a hand and the dust writhed, the specks coalescing into definite, animated shapes. A ribbon of dust transformed into a miniature Karpos, another mote a swath of his cattle.

"Eat, damn you!" the facsimile howled, striking a lowing cow in the side. "Not enough milk, not enough meat—what has gotten into you?"

Limos smirked, dispelling the image with another wave. *Better try asking Demeter for that,* she thought. *Though I'd like to see her try and undo my work.*

The thought of the goddess gave her curious pause. Now that she thought of her, she had never seen what the woman looked like. Any knowledge of Demeter came

11

secondhand, whispered in her ear each night from fervent worshippers seeking Limos's retribution. *Blooming Demeter has been too kind to him and not to me—Food-Giving Demeter brings me less and less each harvest—I have prayed to Earth-Mother Demeter and gotten no answer.* Limos was the second choice. Limos was the contingency plan, the spiteful, spiteful contingency plan.

Demeter was the goal.

Waving an arm, Limos scowled. "Show me her," she demanded the dirt. "So that I may see what is so special."

The dust twitched and squirmed, twisting into the vague shape of a woman. Before any details could form, however, the display collapsed, motionless. With another wave, Limos tried again. Once more the dust trembled, progressing little before coming apart.

Her frown deepened and her nostrils flared. *As the Fates decreed,* she thought. They weren't to meet, even like this. She wiped the dust away with spindly fingers, trying to ignore the disappointment burrowing in her chest. She didn't *actually* care about what the other goddess looked like, did she? When had she ever cared about Demeter as a goddess, much less her appearance? What had she ever given Demeter other than something to combat? She lived to destroy whatever she made flourish—urged the plants to wither and the animals to starve. Did a fox care about the rabbit it ate outside of whatever it got out of its consumption?

It made no sense for her to lament such a thing, and yet, despite all her reasoning, the feeling wouldn't fade.

Another day passed by before the next person arrived.

It had begun to rain that morning, as it so rarely did, turning the barren mountainside into a waste of dark, sticking mud. Limos spent her time indoors, letting the rain hammer incessantly against the stony façade of her abode, her replacement door holding steady in the wake of the watery onslaught.

She curled deeper beneath her covers, the tap-tap-tap-tapping keeping her up despite her efforts. She hardly expected company, nor wanted it. No mortal in their right mind would want to brave climbing a mountain in potentially hazardous conditions as these, even if they did want to speak with her. They were determined creatures, to her understanding, but at some point, the threat of mudslides and death by falling shook most back to their senses.

Most. She supposed in the case of the remaining few, 'heroic' and 'stupid' were synonymous.

"Limos!"

Her dark eyes slid open, ink-black in the darkness of her abode. She didn't recognize the voice. She sighed. Another worshipper, whispering into her ear, no doubt.

"Limos!"

There it was again. Her patchy brows knitted together above her nose. It wasn't coming from her mind like the prayers usually did. She lifted her head from her bed. The wind maybe, or their benefactors, the anemoi. Perhaps Notos and Boreas were playing tricks on her hearing. Already Notos's storms rattled against the mountainside, slicking the earth with water and danger. Despite her presumed contentedness to live out her life so solitarily, every so often the primal, hungry need for company would force her brain into lapses of uncertainty.

"*Limos!*"

She sat up, then stood, knotted hair hanging limply down her back. Not the wind, nor a god of it. Someone was outside, calling her name. Limos cursed under her breath, walking to the door in sluggish steps.

Pushing it open, Limos found the earth already soaked through with cold, sideways-pouring rain. If anything was meant to grow on her land, the waters would have uprooted it. A long-standing, brittle tree had finally loosed itself from the ground, fallen to the muddy, soft earth in a heap of rotted wood and splintered bark. The goddess kept to the doorway, evading most of the spray. She pinned her robes to her body with one hand, lest the wind tear the garments upward and blind her with the fabric.

Some thirty feet away stood the one who called her name. It was a young mountain nymph, an oread, her stone-gray skin and thick, mossy hair soaked with rainwater. Beside her stood a chariot, driven by a pair of dragons. The winged beasts stood at quiet attention, their scales a pale gold like a field of wheat ripe for harvest. Despite their presence in the rain, both the chariot and dragons remained untouched, the droplets repelled whenever they drew near.

Limos's hollow stomach tightened. This was not a mortal problem—not a squabble between petty human farmers about who deserved to eat what and how much. This was a god problem.

At the sight of Limos, the oread squeaked, the noise of terror audible even over the howling wind and pounding rain.

The goddess chuckled. "Can't speak?" Limos asked, humor bleeding into her words. "You were so talkative before."

"I apologize," the nymph said, bowing her head. "I …
I was sent here—"

"By a god, I imagine," Limos said. Her sunken eyes slid
to the chariot. It was so pristine, so unmarred by the
weather, and yet the nymph stood trembling in the cold,
the rain sticking her chiton tight to her slender frame. The
Olympians' kindnesses only ever seemed to go so far.

"By a goddess," the nymph stuttered out. "By
Demeter."

The laughter died in Limos's throat, and her body
locked up. "So that's why," she said, "I'm talking to you
and not her." *Demeter,* she thought, embarrassment
burning her ears. She swallowed thickly, throat bobbing.
Had the goddess somehow known she'd been thinking of
her the day before? She wasn't sure she could explain
herself if she had, nor live down the embarrassment.

The nymph nodded. "She told me the Fates decreed
you should never meet. That they worry you would
destroy one another."

"She told you the truth," Limos concurred. "So tell me,
what is it that Demeter wants from her darker half?"

"Well, she—"

"Come inside, will you?" Limos asked, resting a hand
on her hip. "I'm not going to bite you, and you look
pathetic out in the rain." She gestured with a bony arm to
the inside of her home.

"I shouldn't," the nymph said. "I'm not to stay long."

"I insist," Limos replied. "If Demeter wants my
assistance, she should be willing to wait for it."

Reluctant, the nymph approached, entering the carved
stone home and passing over eroded patches of
footprints. She clung to the wall like a cobweb, but Limos
urged her no further.

"It's quieter in here," Limos said, shutting the door. "I won't have to ask you to repeat yourself."

"Mhm."

Limos sat down on her bed, the weight of her skinny frame barely shaking the seat. "I would give you food, but I rarely need it." Not when humanity's hunger readily fed hers.

"It's alright," the nymph said.

"Then no god can say I haven't offered my hospitality." Sighing, Limos trained her eyes on the girl. "You were saying?"

"A king of Thessaly, Erysichthon, has cut down a great oak in Demeter's sacred groves to build a banquet hall," the nymph related. "In doing so, he killed the dryad who lived within it. Her dying prayers reached Demeter, and now she seeks you to punish him on her behalf."

"Punish a king?" Limos asked. Her broken lips tightened into a razor-thin smile. "I have not punished a *king* in quite a time. It would be a welcome respite from the cows and the trees I am so often asked to ruin instead."

The nymph straightened at the words, her face brightening.

"But," Limos continued, "what has Demeter to offer me, should I help her?"

Sinking back, the nymph's gaze dropped to the stony floor of the cavern. "She said you could ask for whatever you wanted from her, so long as Erysichthon suffered as greatly as possible for his crimes."

Limos's smile threatened to split her gaunt face in half. A million different ideas danced in her mind, but none of them seemed fitting enough or likely to satiate her. Food and wealth would do her no good, no matter how extravagant or great the amount, and she required no beautiful temples nor spots among the self-righteous throngs of Olympians. Love seemed impossible too, without equally divine intervention, and Limos wasn't practiced in the art of sharing her space with another for too long—nor was she certain that she wanted to.

She gasped, realization striking her like a thunderbolt. There was one thing she could ask for, one thing she could not get herself.

"What is your name?" Limos started.

The nymph froze, the only sound between them the thudding of water against the mountain face. "What is my name?"

"Yes, you, messenger. What is your name? You know mine; it is only fair you give yours after bothering to come all this way."

"It's Glaphyra," the girl supplied.

"Well, Glaphyra," Limos continued, "I will punish Erysichthon as requested. In return, I ask that you first give me a tapestry displaying Demeter's image."

"You … y-you want an image of D-Demeter?" Glaphyra asked, stuttering out in disbelief.

"Have her find a weaver to craft it," Limos said, waving a hand. "The greatest and the fastest, if she wants. So long as it is an accurate depiction of her, I will be satisfied, and then the king will suffer."

The oread said nothing at first, but Limos saw in her eyes a flood of relief more powerful than any storm could produce.

"I am certain she can provide that," Glaphyra replied. "W-will that be all?"

Limos nodded. "That will be all. Now, go and tell your goddess what I said, and I will await my masterpiece."

Confirmation was all Glaphyra needed. The nymph darted to the door and rushed back outside, hurrying to the chariot.

Limos shadowed the doorway, calling after her. "Do not forget! Erysichthon suffers only once I acquire that tapestry! Not a moment before!"

Glaphyra gathered the dragons' reins, taking to the air as she lashed them. Before long, both chariot and nymph vanished against the dark skies, swallowed by heavy clouds and rain. Limos watched the storm long after their departure, thoughts swirling.

Demeter, she thought. In due time, she would get to see Demeter.

More importantly, she wondered, how was she to adequately punish a man who had everything?

Days passed and the skies finally cleared, and the pools of water the storms left began to evaporate in their absence. Limos experienced little sleep in the meantime, her mind too occupied with thoughts of the harvest goddess. Vague impressions and silhouettes busied her thoughts, each of them projecting a different potential image.

Olympians could take on many forms, yes, but they usually settled for one when not cavorting with mortals. What would Demeter's be? Would she be tall, she wondered, like a great olive tree full to bursting? Would she be thin like a grapevine, or squat like a gourd? Would her skin be white like cow's milk, or brown like soil, just as soft? Each of them seemed so lovely and untouchable in their own ways.

Her heart beat in a strange, conflicted rhythm. Why did she care? What had prompted her to ask for such a thing? What would the image give her? Peace? Satisfaction? Contentedness at having somehow defied the Fates through her cleverness? Surely not. Her existence was a yearning one, aching and making others ache, always hungering for something different. She didn't think a heart could ache like a stomach could, could yearn to feel in the same, empty way. And yet it hungered and hungered still, famished at the undelivered promise of a glimpse of the goddess.

When not thinking of Demeter, she thought instead of Erysichthon. Already she'd used her scrying dust to peer into his life. His laborers worked quickly, utilizing the fallen dryad's sacred oak to complete the banquet hall. He came and went each day, eating bite after bite, picking from tables that must have spent harvests to fill. The thought of such excess made the goddess's stomach twist. All too often her angry worshippers lamented their starvation, their thirst, their unyielding crops. How many of their meager fruits had gone to waste, rotting as nothing more than a show of wealth as a king sat overfull at his dinner table?

Limos recalled her words to Anakletos. *Hunger is no selective affliction. Even the greatest king still feels its pangs at times.*

Perhaps he needed to feel it more.

Glaphyra returned within the week, the dragons pulling her chariot landing with a roar. Limos hurried out to greet her, and the nymph pulled the rolled-up tapestry out from its spot under her arm.

"Here is your tapestry, as promised," she said. She grabbed one end of the woven piece, beginning to unfurl it so that Limos could see it.

Before her unrolled the woven image of Demeter, and a sharp gasp whistled past Limos's teeth.

She was gorgeous, in the way sunshine after rain was gorgeous—all warm with the promise of renewal. Her pale green robes mingled with the woven flowers at her feet, and Limos couldn't tell where her attire ended and the earth began. Demeter's wheat-gold hair tumbled down her shoulders in thick ringlets, her earth-brown skin dark like overturned soil. Her eyes were a similar vivid brown, set in her skull above full cheeks and plump lips. A crown of proud, upright flowers rested over her temples, their petals rounded and vibrant.

The goddess's frozen gaze beckoned her, and Limos reached out, pressing digits against the image's shoulder. When her fingers brushed the woven canvas, however, the strings began to fray, colors bleeding into duller, muted hues. Limos recoiled, yanking her hand away like the touch had burned her, unable to tear her gaze from the coin-sized spot she had ruined.

"So the Fates intervene once more," she muttered, lips curling into a snarl. She couldn't even have an image of the goddess without worrying that she'd destroy it.

"I-I'm sorry," Glaphyra whispered, glancing back and forth between the tapestry and Limos. "If it means anything, you can barely notice it!"

"Just bring it inside," Limos said, whirling around with a huff. "And hang it for me."

The oread did as instructed, making use of the intermittent protrusions of the well-hewn cave walls. The tapestry hung at eye-level, and Limos stared.

"Is this good?" Glaphyra asked, already at the door.

Limos did not turn her head to regard her. *It is better than good,* she thought. *It is wonderful. It is untouchable.* "Tell Demeter Erysichthon will put his banquet hall to good use," the goddess promised. "Again and again without tire nor satisfaction."

Glaphyra departed, and Limos remained where she stood, staring, craving. Her fingers itched, yearning to grab the tapestry all over, to press her palms into the spots the Fates never wanted her to connect. But each time her eyes wandered to the ruined, shriveled spot, and she stilled her hands.

Who was I trying to fool? she wondered. She thought the image would satisfy her. She *needed* it to satisfy her.

It only made her heart hungrier.

Dissolving into dust again, Limos traveled to Thessaly under cover of night. The formless cloud slipped through the cracks of the palace doors, no attention paid to her presence by the few milling servants still walking the halls. She swept swiftly along the floor into the king's bedchambers, drawing herself into form once inside.

The king slept soundly in his bed, mouth open and snoring. Limos approached him on silent footsteps, the soles of her bare feet leaving a trail of forming prints in the wood. She loomed over the slumbering king, her bony fingers tucking a lock of dark hair behind his ear.

She crouched and leaned in, pressing her lips against his own. Limos breathed into him, filling his stomach with need. Her breath burned his throat on the way down, radiated to his lungs like the biting winds of the desert. Though he might have been dreaming of feasts, she felt his stomach aching, stinging, and lurching.

Limos pulled away from his chapping lips, wiping her mouth with a frayed sleeve. "Eat," she whispered. "And never stop."

A servant opened the door, but she was long gone.

Weeks passed, and Limos watched her work progress. She sat in her home, urging her scrying dust to show her Erysichthon. It leaped to attention, swirling into his banquet hall, his plates, and the king himself. Dust took the shape of breads, cheeses drizzled with honey, quail eggs, salted fish. It all passed his lips, sitting insatiably in the king's stomach as he attempted to wash his meal down with krater after krater of watered-down wine. Before long, he would request another feast, but still his efforts were for naught. Still his stomach ached, clawing itself to pieces with lion-like ferocity. The banquets came faster, tall piles growing smaller in their frequency.

Every time he would eat his fill, Limos would glance to the tapestry. She searched the frozen eyes for approval, eager for a glimmer of confirmation.

"We work so well together, don't you think?" she asked the false Demeter. "Your harvests, my hunger."

Erysichthon worsened in his plight. All his wealth went to food. He sent away his servants, stripped his palace of its furnishings and decoration and sold them. Sold them, bought food. Ate. Hungered. Sold them, bought food.

Ate. Hungered. Sold them, sold them, sold them, until the once great palace lay in unattended ruin, bare and shell-like. And all the while, the pockets of toiling farmers grew heavy with the king's patronage.

Erysichthon sold his own daughter, Mestra, to the first man he could find. The girl wept and prayed to the gods for salvation, and Limos saw them intervene on behalf of one of their human lovers. They gave her the ability to change shape, and she fled her husband-to-be in disguise. The king abused this, selling her again and again, letting her return each time as something different; a mare, a doe, a fisherman—but never a wife, helpless to watch her father eat her bride price at the banquet table. Finally, the dust facsimile of the king's daughter grew wings and fled, and Limos could not help but laud her.

At long last, there was nothing to sell. He tried to pawn off his palace, but no one would buy it in the state it was in. He gnawed at his covers night after night, tearing them to little pieces with his worn-away teeth until his bed was just another plate he'd picked clean. He bit into his fingers, tearing flesh from bone, swallowing viscera and blood like bread and water. He disappeared down his own throat, shrinking into voracious nothing. When the Thessalians finally braved the silent castle, they found only a pile of blood and scattered bones in the king's bedchamber.

Limos gave the tapestry another glance, her smile just as ravenous as the disappearing king's.

What did the Fates know?

With her retribution done, the days passed as they always did, sluggish like solidifying mud. The rush of excitement ebbed away, leaving her alone and restless once more.

The winds picked up on the mountainside one evening, colder than she remembered them being. Their frigid breezes swept past the underside of her door, shaking the tapestry and prickling bumps along her bony arms. She took refuge under her covers, waiting for the winds to stop.

Limos waited day after day, but the world only grew colder. One day, she poked her head past her front door and found that the rain was different. It was *wrong*. It was cold like the incessant wind, swirled about in the air in little white puffs of frozen water. It stuck to the ground in a sheet of slush-like powder, dampening the earth before seizing it up again. She slammed the door closed and waited for the normal rain to return, to no avail.

Soon, the words of her worshippers came, frantic and confused.

Ever-Hungry Limos, my crops are freezing where they stand.

Famine-Maker Limos, Demeter has forsaken me.

Wasting Limos, I am just as hungry as you.

The goddess remained in bed, nourished by her pleas, trying to ignore the formation of her newest hunger— curiosity. What could be doing this to the rain? To her mountain? Was it happening everywhere? Surely it must be, for her worshippers spoke in her ear from all over, weeping.

Limos, I am starving.

Limos, Demeter despises us.

Limos, nothing grows.

Limos, make the hunger stop.

Limos, I am dying.

In her equal confusion, she could answer none of them.

It wasn't much longer until someone knocked on her door.

Limos had been waiting for a human to approach her ever since the strange rains had begun. Braving the elements to speak to her didn't seem as foolish as it did before, now that the world was under the strange, cold grip of what she could only assume to be an angry god.

"Who is it?" Limos asked, keeping her body pressed against her cot.

An older woman's voice answered, tired and shaking. "Can you speak to Hades?"

The question stunned her into silence. *Hades?* The god of the underworld? Since when was his domain her business, save her hunger shepherding mortals into his arms?

"I am not Hades," Limos replied. "Who is asking?"

"Demeter."

Limos frowned. "Another messenger?" she asked. The voice didn't *sound* like Glaphyra's.

"No, Limos. I came here myself."

Her sunken eyes threatened to drop from her skull in surprise. She launched herself out of bed, nearly tripping over her long garments as she rushed to the door. Limos forced the wooden panel open, pushing aside inches of cold, white fluff.

Demeter looked … normal, for lack of a better word. The tapestry was but a single static image in comparison to the goddess before her, and yet it felt more divine than she. Her earth-brown skin was dull, her wet, wheat-gold hair shot through with stressed streaks of silver. Age lines plowed rows of wrinkles across her full cheeks, and deep bags hung beneath her dark eyes. Her garments were soiled at the bottom with mud, spotted with frozen flakes of what used to be rain, and the wreath of flowers at her forehead was drooping and withered.

Limos's wasting stomach tightened, and she resisted the urge to stomp and seethe like an unruly child. After all her wanting, she was here. So why was it not enough? Why was she not what she wanted? Where was the woman from the tapestry? Where was the proud goddess who made the world spring up with life? Where was Earth-Mother Demeter, Blooming, Food-Giving Demeter?

She looked back into the goddess's brown eyes, and she realized. She knew that look from anywhere—would recognize the bags and the downturned lips and the anticipating silence of her gaze. It was hunger—not for food, but something equally important.

"Why are you here?" Limos finally asked.

"Can you speak to Hades?" Demeter repeated.

"Whatever for?"

The harvest goddess's eyes dropped to the covered earth, closing lids sending tears down her cheeks. She sucked in a breath, her quick, sputtering exhale fogging the air in front of her. "He's taken my daughter," she said. "He's taken Kore."

Limos's patchy brows darted up her forehead. "Taken her? You mean—"

"No," Demeter cut her off. "No, she isn't dead. I would know. He took her. Stole her from me. I heard her screaming and … the nearby nymphs told me when I went to find her." Her shoulders trembled like someone had placed the heavens upon them. "He opened the earth and dragged her down with him, and now I am alone."

"Oh, Demeter," Limos said, frowning.

"Apollo saw it from his chariot. He told me Zeus arranged the abduction. Said it wasn't for a mother to worry about her daughter's marriage—her marriage—so long as it happened at all. That's how the mortals have always done it. I ... I tried to get him to talk to Hades—to make him reconsider, but he refused." She squeezed her eyes shut tighter, muscles bulging in her jaw. "I have gone to every god and goddess I can, trying to make them move for me, but each of them refuses."

"And so you came to me," Limos whispered.

Demeter's eyes slid open, bloodshot from her weeping. "I can't bring myself to make anything grow," the goddess lamented. "I have no more reason to. It feels as though I have lost the world ten times over, and there is nothing I can do to restore it."

The goddess fell silent again, and Limos watched, equally speechless. It was true, mortal wives rarely had a say in who their daughters married, but Limos would have thought the Olympians would have been above such a practice. She chewed the inside of her cheek, Demeter's soft sobs and the whipping winds the only sounds between them as she pondered.

"What can I do?" Demeter wept.

No one came to her for kindness, Limos thought. But perhaps, just once in her life, she could provide it. "Shelter here," Limos finally suggested. "Here the ground never bears fruit, and no roots cling deep in the soil. Far be it from me to ask you to make things grow and flourish— not before, not now. I never needed any of it."

"We were never to meet," Demeter lamented, reddened gaze drifting back in the direction of the whitened mountainside. "The Fates insisted. I shouldn't be here. I-I only came because there was no one else to go to."

Limos's cracked lips curled up at the corners, a sad laugh rumbling in her skinny throat before she could stop herself. "And you were never to neglect your duties," she reminded, gesturing to the land beyond. "What is one more broken promise?"

"Surely you would destroy me. Just your touch would make me yearn, make me hungry and desperate."

"Look at yourself," Limos said, the response harsher than she meant it to be. "Look at the world. The rain has frozen, the earth covered in its vast whiteness. Nothing grows in your grief. I do not have to make you yearn, Demeter. You are already yearning."

Demeter's bleary eyes met Limos's sunken gaze. "You are right," she said.

"Then live here, and I will yearn with you," Limos offered, stepping back so that the other could walk inside. "Like the rest of the world. I need no sustenance as humans do. I can wait. Their hunger nourishes me like your harvests nourish them. Until your daughter returns, I can be your company."

Demeter hovered in the doorway, feet in the threshold. "But what if he never brings her back to me?" she asked.

Limos's lips spread into a thin smirk. "Olympians love their sacrifices. If the crops and the animals die, so too will the sacrifices. When that happens, they will turn to you to restore it, and you may make whatever demand of them you please."

"And if they say no?"

Determination flashed in her dark gaze. "Trust in me, Demeter. No one, man or god, says no when he is hungry enough."

The other goddess's lips curled into a tiny smile, and with a withered vine she pulled the door closed behind her.

The days passed, and then weeks. Kore showed no signs of return, and Demeter's frozen rain continued to batter the countryside. It piled up over the earth, burying palaces, farms, and forests in equal measure. The mortals gave it a name—snow—just so they could bemoan its existence in their unanswered prayers.

All the while, Limos and Demeter remained sequestered in the former's mountain abode. It was overwhelming at first, having to share her space with another, but the feeling melted away with time. Before long, Limos brightened every time she heard the other's footsteps or soft snores. It was a strange familiarity, one that filled her heart and stomach with equal warmth.

Every so often they would sit together on Limos's cot, chatting endlessly. As immortals of such differing domains, there was never a shortage of topics to discuss, nor stories to share. Demeter told her of a king she once turned into a lynx for trying to kill one of her worshippers, and Limos told her of her punishment for Erysichthon.

"I see you still have that tapestry up to show for it," Demeter said, eyes flitting to the woven image.

Limos shrugged. "It's a work of art."

Demeter huffed. "It's *embellished*."

"Both things can be true."

"I suppose so." Demeter smiled, but the expression just as quickly faltered. Limos wanted to snatch the curve of her lips up and trap it in a jar so that the world and time and sadness might not wither it.

But if Demeter needed no comfort, what use would Limos be?

The first god came after a month of no growth. Demeter hid at Limos's request, venturing deep into the mountain while the goddess opened the door.

"Limos," the god outside began. It was Apollo, all bright hair and bronze skin. "I've come to speak to Demeter."

"Have you come with Kore?" Limos asked.

"I have not."

"She won't speak with you until she's back, you know," Limos said.

"It's not up to me."

"Then why are you here?

Apollo froze, the ever-present sunlight of his gaze smothered by invisible storm clouds. "I was there when it happened," he said. "I thought that would make her talk to me. If not, I had been hoping you would convince her to return to Olympus and answer her worshipper's prayers."

"I'm not certain where you gathered that hope from," Limos replied. "But it is misplaced. Talk to Hades instead. Demeter has her terms, and I will not move them. I am the goddess of starvation, not compromise."

The last thing Limos saw of Apollo was his scowl, and then the door closed in his face. A blast of heat filled the vicinity, and the Sun god vanished just as quickly as he'd come.

"He's gone," Limos said, turning to regard the inside of her home.

Demeter poked her head back into view, her lips trembling up at the corners.

Limos smiled back.

It became a routine, dealing with the Olympians. Where Apollo came, Dionysus followed, then Athena, then Poseidon. Each time they refused to listen, and each time Limos spurned their pleas, urging them to go to Hades if they truly wished this 'winter' to end. And each night the two would climb into bed together and wait out the prayers and pleas, their looping bodies the only warm things in the entire world.

Limos, we are tired.

Limos was awake.

Limos, we are hungry.

Limos was fulfilled.

Limos, we are dying.

Limos had never felt more alive.

Demeter never came apart at her touch, not like the tapestry, not like the scrying dust. Whenever Limos touched her, she only curled deeper, embrace tightening with certain vivacity. In the darkness, Limos threaded her bony fingers through the goddess's hair, trailing and pressing her chapped lips up her neck, on her nose, her cheek, her lips.

The only thing that pulled them apart was the sound of booming thunder, powerful and deafening as though a cloud hovered right outside their door. Limos unhooked herself from the goddess, leaping out of bed in a rush of limbs.

"Who is it?" she asked, though she already knew.

"Zeus," a man's voice replied. The name came out in a growl, rumbling like the thunder he conjured.

Limos turned her head to Demeter, gesturing with her chin. The gold-haired goddess, retreated under the covers, pressing herself flat against the bed to obscure her shape from view. With Demeter sufficiently hidden, Limos pushed open the door.

Zeus towered over her immediately, eyes storming and dark hair peppered with ever-falling flakes.

"Come to bargain?" Limos asked.

"Come to *inform*," the king of gods corrected, "that Demeter has forced our hands."

"Oh?" Though she kept the amusement out of her voice, the smug satisfaction flooded Limos's body with excitement.

"We cannot rule over a world without life," Zeus declared. "And so, I have sent Hermes to fetch Kore."

A gasp erupted from behind Limos, and Demeter staggered out of bed, discarding any attempts to hide herself from the greater god's view. "Will she be here soon?" Demeter asked, shrinking in a hunch beneath Zeus's gaze.

"As soon as Hermes can return from the underworld."

Demeter swallowed, taking a deep, shaking breath. She reached out, slipping her hand into Limos's and lacing their fingers together.

Limos gave her hand a reassuring squeeze, dark eyes flicking to the goddess before returning to Zeus. "I am happy to hear."

"I will be *happier*," Zeus cut in, "when things grow again."

Demeter straightened out of her hunch. "When my daughter comes," she insisted. "Not a moment before."

Limos grinned. To hear determination rooted so deeply in Demeter's words ... she couldn't help but feel proud of her.

Such feelings of pride, however, quickly fell to the wayside.

Hermes arrived in a rush of winged feet, touching down on the snowy earth. He carried Demeter's daughter in his arms, holding her tight against his chest. The girl wasn't happy. Waves of already shed tears stained her face, shining in the light reflected off the snow. Her dark hair was a mess, tugged this way and that, and her lower lip wobbled.

"Kore!" Demeter gasped. She rushed outside to reach Hermes, snow crunching beneath her. Where her feet landed the powder melted, returning the earth once more to barren, damp mundanity.

"Mother," Kore spoke up. Her voice warbled like a bird's, her song anything but cheerful.

Hermes helped the girl to her feet, holding her shoulders steady so that she could regain her balance.

"I was so worried," Demeter said, throwing her arms around her child. "I thought for certain I wouldn't see you again."

Whatever meager dam the girl had created for Demeter broke, and she burst into tears again. "Mother, I'm sorry!" Kore sobbed. She wrapped her arms around the goddess, fingers digging deep.

"What is there to be sorry for?" Demeter asked, pulling away just enough to wipe the girl's tears.

While Kore responded only in blubbers, Hermes cleared his throat. "Before she left," he explained, "she ate fruit from the underworld."

Demeter tore away from her daughter, whirling on her heels to face the messenger god. "She *what?!*"

Hermes threw his hands up in surrender. "It's what he told me!"

"He tricked me!" Kore wept. "He—he said it was a parting gift—I … I was so hungry, I'd forgotten the rules … I wasn't thinking!" She covered her face with her hands, fingers muffling her words. "I was stupid, so stupid!"

"No," Limos cut in. She pushed through the melted path Demeter had carved, approaching the younger goddess. "You are *not* stupid. You were hungry. You had been in the underworld for what, months? Mortals cannot survive *days* without food. You were homesick and you missed your mother. Your hunger wasn't a crime."

"Even so," Zeus said. "Mortals who eat of the underworld's fruits are bound to stay there forever."

"She is not a mortal," Demeter said. "Surely something can be done! I've just gotten her back; I will *not* lose her again!"

"We cannot let the humans suffer any longer," Hermes agreed. "Any more of this winter and they will all die!"

Zeus rubbed his chin in thought, and the rest fell silent. Only the snow and the wind filled the quiet, whispering like little suggestions. It felt like a month, two months, a year more of barren winter, but he finally spoke. "Perhaps," he began, "an arrangement can be made."

"A-an arrangement?" Demeter echoed. "What sort of arrangement?"

"You may have her," Zeus began, "for half the year. For the remainder, she will return to the underworld to be with Hades."

Kore wailed and Demeter's eyes flashed with anger. "You can't possibly mean to send her back!"

Zeus stood firm. "She knew the rules."

The harvest goddess's lips pulled back in a snarl, and she whipped her head from Zeus, to Limos, to Zeus again. "If she goes back, so too does the cold and the snow. So too does the hunger."

Zeus sighed. "The mortals will have to adjust, then. I see no other compromise Hades will accept."

Demeter huffed, breath coming out in a cloud. "But she stays with me now. Come for her later. I have more than earned my time with her."

Zeus waved a hand. "Very well."

Demeter's eyes softened at the concession, and she turned back to Limos. "I won't forget this," she breathed. "What you've done, just to let me see her again. I won't."

Limos's smile warmed. "My door is always open for you," she said. "But for now, you and your daughter should focus on one another."

Demeter closed the distance between them with certain steps, stopping only once she and Limos were inches apart. She leaned close, her whispering words warming Limos's ear. "I will be back," she promised. "When he takes her, the snow will fall again, and I will make my way to you."

A short, hoarse chuckle rumbled in Limos's throat, and she nodded. "I will wait for you, Fates be damned. I always have."

One by one, the gods vanished into the clearing skies, Zeus as a storm cloud, Hermes on his winged sandals, and the mother and daughter pair as a stream of multicolored petals. The petals ribboned through the air with the graceful fluidity of a serpent, disappearing against the shining sun.

Limos searched the skies for them long after they were gone, and her heart began to hunger once more.

The humans called it 'spring', and Limos couldn't have come up with a better name if she tried. The snow melted away, the earth reappearing first in patches, then gigantic swaths of well-moistened mud. For a short while, the path that Demeter had walked on her way to greet Kore budded with wildflowers, their short stems and petaled heads bobbing in the wind. Soon enough though, the barrenness reclaimed the mountainside, and the flowers withered into dust.

The humans thanked the gods—including Limos—for the winter's end with abundant sacrifices, but no cow or sheep or libation offered ever filled the void in her heart. She ate and drank her gifts alone, accompanied only by the woven image of Demeter that still hung on her wall and the silence of the mountain.

She looked up at the tapestry and scowled. Demeter was right. It *was* embellished. What she wouldn't have given to keep the goddess there with her forever, imperfections and all.

The warm months passed humanity by, and then the snow began again. The howling winds and falling flakes failed to frighten her as they used to. Now, Limos listened to the whipping air, letting it play tricks on her mind, letting it speak to her in scattered, impossible voices.

"Limos!" Demeter, the *real* Demeter, called at last.

Limos threw open her door to the goddess, spotting the petals touching down in the distance. She hurried back inside, seizing the tapestry from her cavern's wall. She understood it now as the false Demeter unraveled at her touch. The Fates weren't worried they would destroy each other. They were worried they would empower each other.

The ruined threads fell to the floor in a twisted heap, and Limos looked to the approaching goddess with a smile.

It was going to be a long winter.

Acknowledgements

If I were to thank every single person who had the slightest hand in shaping me into the writer I am today, we would be here for a week. I'll spare you the encyclopedia and give you the highlights instead:

The biggest thank yous go out to my mom, dad, grammy, grandfather, and my two lovely siblings Chiara and Jack. You believed in me when it seemed no one else did, and cheered me on through thick and thin.

Thank you, Dan, who remains my champion even as I venture into the wild indie world. You're always the one I come to for advice, a punny joke, or both.

Thank you, Marcy, Gavin, Xander, Jasper, Ender, Damien, Esme, and Matty, for keeping me company on voice calls while I was trying to work—yes, even the ones that went on way too long and lasted until way too late. Especially those.

Thank you to the wonderful people on the Brigid's Gate Press team for making sure *Food for Thought* was in perfect shape for her debut. I'm so sorry about all the commas.

Thank you, Elizabeth Leggett, for creating this incredible, utterly beautiful cover! Seriously, I still can't stop staring at it. You, reading this, look at the cover again! It's gorgeous!

And lastly, thank you, for choosing to take a chance on Limos. I can only hope she sticks with you as she's stuck with me, for better or worse.

ABOUT THE AUTHOR

Ariana Ferrante is an #actuallyautistic college student, playwright, and speculative fiction author. Her main interests include reading and writing fantasy and horror of all kinds, featuring heroes big and small getting into all sorts of trouble. She has been published by Eerie River Publishing and Soteira Press, among others. On the playwriting side, her works have been featured in the Kennedy Center American College Theater Festival, and nominated for national awards. She currently lives in Florida, but travels often, both for college and leisure. You may find her on Twitter at @ariana_ferrante, and on Instagram at @arianaferrantebooks.

CONTENT WARNINGS

Animal death
Body horror
Cannibalism
Gore
Kidnapping (mentioned)
Starvation (mentioned)

More From Brigids Gate Press

Medusa.
Cursed by the gods.
Slain by Perseus.
A monster.

So the poets sang.

The poets got it wrong.

Daughter of Sarpedon: A Tempered Tales Collection is an anthology of short stories, poems, and drabbles, ranging from retellings to completely new stories, from ancient to modern day.

Featuring the talents of Eva Papasoulioti, Laura G. Kaschak, Linda D. Addison, SJ Townend, Christina Sng, Ann Wuehler, Amanda Steel, Ellie Detzler, Elizabeth Davis, Katherine Silva, Megan Baffoe, Rachel Horak Dempsey, Romy Tara Wenzel, Stephanie M. Wytovich, Die Booth, Rachel Rixen, Federica Santini, Thomas Joyce, L. Minton, Catherine McCarthy, Ai Jiang, Katie Young, Lyndsey Croal, Elyse Russell, Deborah Markus, April Yates, Theresa Derwin, Jason P. Burnham, Claire McNerney, Marisca Pichette, Gordon Linzner, Patricia Gomes, Stephen Frame, Sharmon Gazaway, Kayla Whittle, Alexis DuBon, Sam Muller, Avra Margariti, Christina Bagni, Kristin Cleaveland, Eric J. Guignard, Marshall J. Moore, Owl Goingback, Renée Meloche, Cindy O'Quinn, Eugene Johnson, Alyson Faye, Jeanne Bush, and Agatha Andrews.

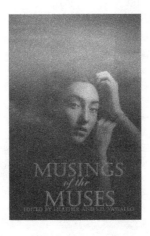

Sing O Muse, of the rage of Medusa, cursed by gods and feared by men …

From the mists of time, and ages past,
The muses have gathered; hear now their songs.

A web of revenge spun 'neath the moon;
A poet's wife who breaks her bonds;
A warrior woman on a quest of honor;
A painful lesson for a treacherous heart;
A goddess and a mortal, bound together by the travails of motherhood.

And more.

Listen to the muses, as they sing aloud … HER story.

Musings of the Muses, 65 stories and poems based on Greek myths, is an anthology of monsters, heroines, and goddesses, ranging from ancient Greece to modern day America. They, like the myths themselves, cast long shadows of horror, fantasy, love, betrayal, vengeance, and redemption. This anthology revisits those old tales and presents them anew, from her point of view.dangerous place to live.

Who are we if not for the monsters that we keep?

They Hide: Short Stories to Tell in the Dark collects thirteen chilling tales that weave through the shadows, exploring the nature of fear, powerlessness, and control.

- A series of murders in a New England colony
- An untamed beast in pre-revolutionary France
- A mysterious stranger who invades 18th-century Ireland
- A traveling circus that takes more than the price of admission
- A gathering of the Dark, telling tales on the longest night of the year, and more.

Come play with vampires, werewolves, ghosts, zombies, ghouls and the devil himself. Make sure you check under the bed and don't turn out the lights.

The settlement of Grey's Bluffs is a prosperous town. An independent community dwelling in the shadows of the mountains known only as The Hungers.

Esther Foxman and Siobhan O'Clery have grown up in Grey's Bluffs, thriving out on the western territories in the aftermath of the Civil War. Devoted to one another and their home, the two set out to complete a regular pact at the Hungers to ensure that Grey's Bluffs continues to prosper.

Cyril Redstone is a man who knows death well. Becoming a mercenary after the Civil War, Cyril leads the marauding Blackhawks from one slaughter to the next. Hired to destroy Grey's Bluffs, Cyril cares little for morality, nor that he owes its founder his life.

Esther and Siobhan are left to defend the only home they have ever known from the Blackhawks, their confrontation driving them deep into the mountains.

Where the darkest secrets of the Hungers await them.

Visit our website at: www.brigidsgatepress.com

Printed in the USA
CPSIA information can be obtained
at www.ICGtesting.com
LVHW091101071123
763047LV00058B/823

9 781957 537856